C L

F
Yam
c.1

Yamaguchi, Tohr
Two crabs and the
moonlight

Date Due

MONTAGUE		
KLA. R B 4 2 2 '74		
MONTA 49 1 3 '74		
GREN D - 1 - 6 '76		
DORR E 1 0 4 '78		
BUTTE A 8 3 0 '77		
DORR G 9 - 5 - '78		
SEIAD B 1 1 2 9 '79		
MONTA F 4 - 9 '80		
KLA. R B 9 - 8 - '80		

MACDO B 1 1 2 n '80

6029

When a mother crab is caught in a net,
her son offers even his life if the moon will
save her.

#6029

Two Crabs and the Moonlight

Books by Tohr Yamaguchi
Two Crabs and the Moonlight
The Golden Crane

Two Crabs
and the Moonlight

by Tohr Yamaguchi

Illustrations by Marianne Yamaguchi

Holt, Rinehart and Winston   New York / Chicago / San Francisco

To Thérèse Kaspensen
Copenhagen, Denmark

The fall was deep, leaves of the mountains turning red, orange, yellow, and brown. The sky was indigo to the end of infinity and the air was clear. The sweet fragrance of chrysanthemums was everywhere, their white petals falling on the stony brook that ran gurgling by.

Behind a rock in the brook were two river crabs; the small crab was Åke and the larger one was his mother.

"Mother, let's go over to the other side of the brook," said Åke. "I see the green moss."

These small crabs ate the river moss that grew over the round surface of the rocks. They swam sideways, but skillfully, from one rock to another in the clear water that looked soft in the sunshine. And when the night fell, they hid themselves in the shadow of the rocks, their near-sighted eyes sleeping inside their shells.

"Yes, Åke, I will go first and you follow me," said his mother, shaking her small pincers. "Be careful, though, the current is very swift!"

They went to the other side of the brook, where
the water ran whirling around a large rock that blocked
the main stream. The bottom of the brook was covered
with pebbles, white and black, and also many acorns
that fell from oak trees and sank into the water.

"Mother, look over there!" said Åke, as he stopped
eating the moss they had found covering the rock like
a green carpet. "I see a wooden basket by the rock
there."

Yes, deep in the water there was a bottle-shaped wooden basket, which farmers often used to trap fish and crabs in the brook. Usually they placed some potatoes or a bundle of river moss into the basket to attract the fish and crabs, and once the prey was inside, they would never be able to come out — until the farmers came back to catch the poor frightened fish and crabs.

"No, no, Åke, don't go near it!" his mother warned him, knowing the danger of such traps. She had seen many crabs, including her husband, captured in them. So, they swam back again to the other side of the brook and prepared to go home, as the sun had already set behind the mountains. But unfortunately there was a very wise farmer, living near the brook, who had seen a white fish net while visiting a market in town. He thought it would catch more fish and crabs than a

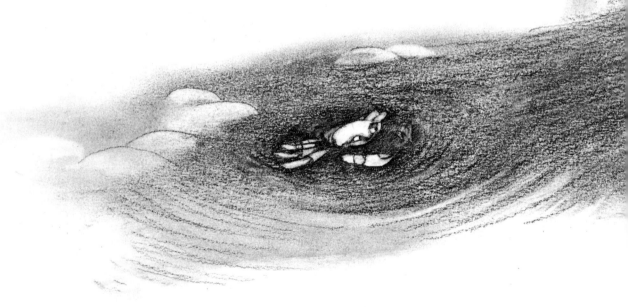

wooden basket, because they would find it hard to see in the swift current of the brook. And so his fish net was hiding in the stream as the crabs swam toward the other side.

"Oh! I didn't see this!" exclaimed the mother crab, her legs caught by the net, while Åke slipped through. He was much smaller.

"Oh, Mother!" cried Åke. "I'll come and cut the net with my pincers!"

"No, no, Åke, stay where you are," the mother crab called, struggling to get out of the net. "Your pincers are too fragile, and the net will catch you, too." The day was dark now and they could hardly see each other. Only the white bubbles of the brook stood out against the darkness.

"Oh, Mother, what can I do to help you!" Åke
cried, his long eyes filling with tears.

"Don't worry, Åke," said his mother, trying to
comfort him—though she, too, was afraid that she
would be caught by the farmer in the morning. "I'll get
out of this soon."

The round full moon had risen from the mountains, throwing her long silver light over the earth, sound asleep and quiet. The light fell over the stream, still running and gurgling, and over the mother crab, caught in the tangling fish net. And over little Åke, sad and tired, who cried and cried.

"Why are you crying so hard?" the moonlight asked Åke.

Åke looked up into the moonlight. "Because my mother is caught in a net, that's why!"

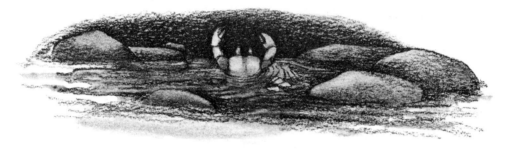

"Why don't you help her, then?" the moonlight asked him.

"I can't," Åke answered, sad and sobbing. "The net's too strong for my pincers; not even a great carp was able to help her when he passed by here about two hours ago, not even a beautiful water lily which went floating downstream!"

The moonlight said nothing.

"Could you help my mother?" Åke asked the moonlight.

"Yes, perhaps I can — but on conditions," answered the moonlight coldly.

"Then, please, if you will help us, I'll do anything you ask," Åke promised desperately.

"Wait a minute," the moonlight said calmly. "You must agree to the conditions before I will do anything."

"What are the conditions?" Åke asked impatiently.

"Well, first, you must give me both of your pincers," proposed the moonlight, "so that I can use them as scissors to cut silk and make my dresses."

Pincers are very important to crabs, because they are always used for swimming in the rapid current, clinging to rocks, and above all picking the river moss. But Åke wanted to help his mother, so he said, "You shall have my pincers if you can help my mother out of the net."

"Well, that's very good. Now I can sew." And the moonlight was delighted. "But that's not the only thing I want. I also want your long eyes, because with them I could see the whole earth to the smallest detail."

Eyes are very important to crabs, because without them they have no other way to know their surroundings. Even though they can feel with their legs, it is actually their eyes that see and feel their surroundings best of all. Well, Åke would have neither pincers nor eyes if his mother was to be rescued, but he wanted desperately to save his mother.

"All right, you shall have my eyes, too, if you can

help my mother," answered Åke to the moonlight,
which was shining upon the pebbles of the brook.

"But I have one more thing you must promise,"
said the moonlight, as if she had not asked poor Åke for
enough already. "I would like your shiny black shell
to make a ring for my finger."

But, oh, it would bring death to tiny Åke to give his shell to the moonlight, because after his mother would be safe out of the net he would have neither his pincers, nor his eyes, nor his shell. But Åke loved his mother very much and wanted her to be saved, even if

he had to lose his own life. Yet he was very frightened.

"No, Åke, don't listen to the moonlight," shouted his mother, "don't make any promises—I'll be all right tomorrow morning!"

"But I don't want you to die, Mother," answered little Åke, his eyes filled with tears. "The moonlight will have all she has been promised, and you'll be safe!"

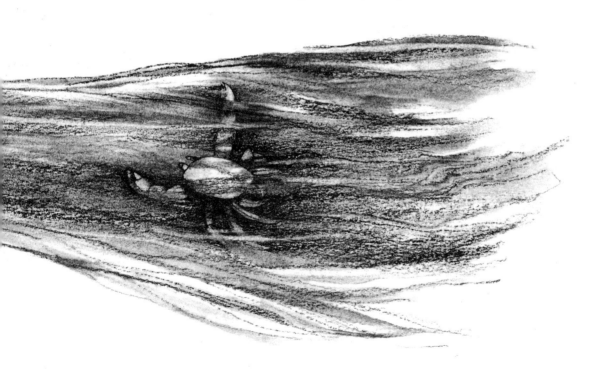

So, the moonlight went over to Åke's mother, and in about half an hour untangled the net and cut the mother crab free. The mother crab swam to Åke and embraced him. And they both cried. But then Åke realized that the moonlight was waiting for him to keep his promises.

"Well, Mother, the moonlight is waiting for me,"
Åke said in a low voice.

"No, Åke, you stay here." His mother seized his
leg. "I'll give my pincers, and my eyes, and my shell to
the moonlight."

"No, Mother, you mustn't!" Åke tried to get out of his mother's grasp. "I promised the moonlight in order to save you—not for you to save me!"

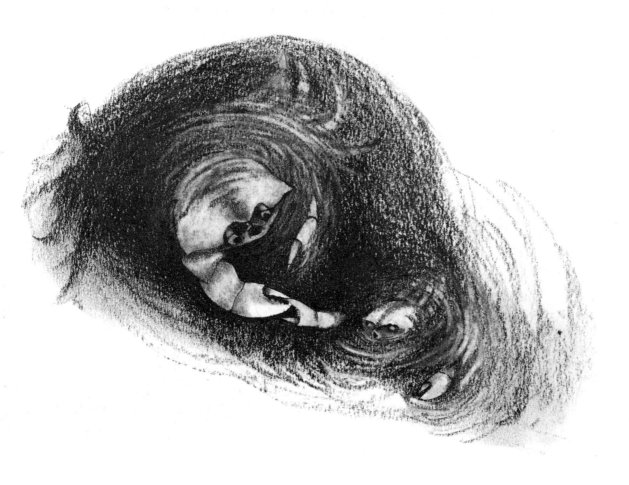

"Now, now, listen," said the moonlight. "I want none of your pincers, nor your eyes, nor your shell— all I wanted was to see if Åke really wished to help his mother and was really brave enough to do something about it. I don't want any of the things you promised,

but, instead, won't you and your mother come and live in the moon with me? You will have a large brook all to yourselves, safe from any farmer's trap, and you'll live for many hundreds of years very happily."

Åke and his mother accepted the moonlight's invitation, and perhaps you will see, when you look very carefully into the full moon, the two crabs swimming across the brook, eating the river moss, and playing with the acorns.

About the Author

TOHR YAMAGUCHI, born in Tokyo, comes from a musical family. From his father, an orchestral conductor, and his mother, a vocal recitalist, he learned the rich stories recounted in European music. In kindergarten and elementary school he re-told these song-tales to his schoolmates and was known as a "foreign story" teller. In high school, he began to write short stories and plays. Mr. Yamaguchi received his college education in the United States where he now lives and continues to write while working as a demographer. Author of *The Golden Crane*, a Japanese folktale, he now turns to this story of his own invention, inspired while bicycling home one moonlit night and written as a kind of relaxation from his studies at the Princeton Graduate School.

About the Artist

MARIANNE YAMAGUCHI, a graduate in painting and illustration from the Rhode Island School of Design, was also the illustrator of *The Golden Crane*. Mrs. Yamaguchi is soon to apprentice in the art of woodcut print in Kyoto, Japan, where she and her husband and their young daughter plan to visit next year.